D0281422

Happy Birthday
Giidh!

Love David +
Stephanie xt

To Jon and Tom - M.M. and N.S.

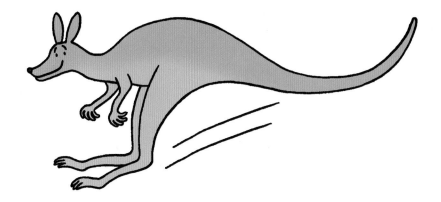

First published 2010 by Macmillan Children's Books
This edition published 2015 by Macmillan Children's Books
an imprint Pan Macmillan
20 New Wharf Road, London N1 9RR
Associated companies throughout the world
www.panmacmillan.com

ISBN: 978-1-5098-0141-1

Text copyright © Michaela Morgan 2010 and 2015
Illustrations copyright © Nick Sharratt 2010 and 2015
Moral rights asserted.

All rights reserved. No part of this publication may be reproduced, stored in or
introduced into a retrieval system, or transmitted in any form, or by any means,
(electronic, mechanical, photocopying, recording or otherwise) without the prior
written permission of the publisher.

1 3 5 7 9 8 6 4 2

A CIP catalogue for this book is available from the British Library.

Printed in China

NEVER SHAKE A RATTLESNAKE

Written by Michaela Morgan

Illustrated by Nick Sharratt

MACMILLAN CHILDREN'S BOOKS

You should never tuck **piranhas** inside your best pyjamas.

Don't try to knit a scarf for an extra-tall giraffe

You should never style the hair of a grumpy grizzly **bear.**

STYLING MOUSSE

You should never NEVER
shake a rattlesnake.

Don't nest up high in trees

with the **hairy** chimpanzees

and don't try to keep
a whale in a lake.

Don't lend your **hat** and **coat** to a goat.

Don't try to dress a fox
in **frilly** bonnet
and pink socks

and don't EVER take
a rhino on a boat.

Don't picnic with a **python** in the park.

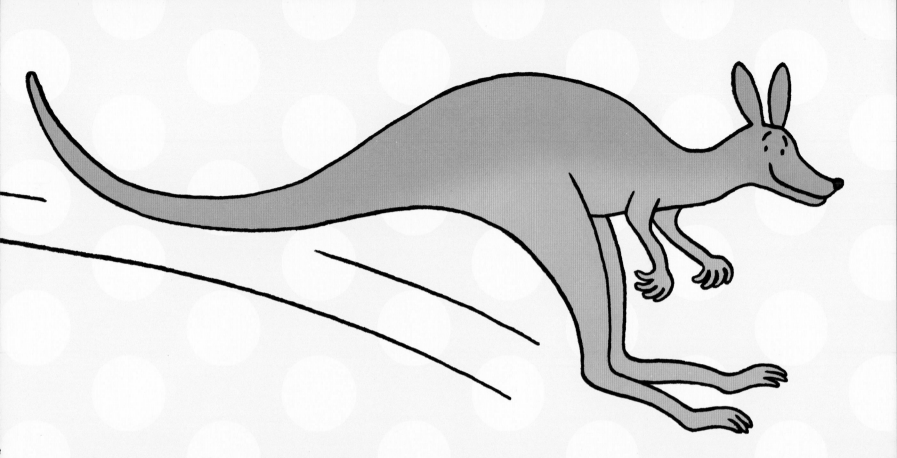

DON'T keep a chameleon in the **dark**.

and don't leave tiny dogs out in the **breeze**.

Don't buy **fancy** shoes for camels . . .

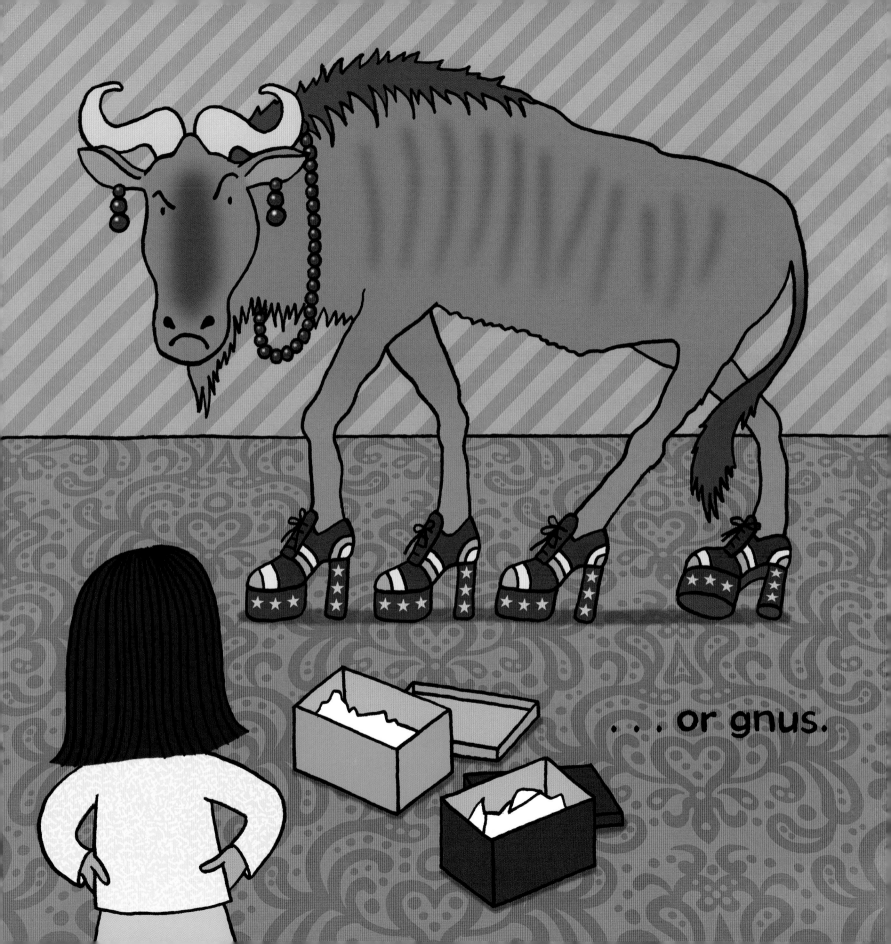

. . . or gnus.

and never

never

sneeeeeze!

ATCHOO!